"It'll do all the washing and cooking and shopping – everything! All the bits I'm no good at!" said Mum. "You'll have to recharge it sometimes, that's all!"

"Er, Mum . . ." I said.

Mum beamed. "So, it's all decided then!"

"Well . . ." I thought about it. Perhaps it *would* be nice to have things organized for a change. And a real robot around . . . how cool would that be?

"OK," I said.

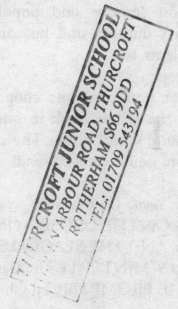

YOUNG CORGI BOOKS

Young Corgi books are perfect when you are looking for great books to read on your own. They are full of exciting stories and entertaining pictures. There are funny books, scary books, spine-tingling stories and mysterious ones. Whatever your interests you'll find something in Young Corgi to suit you: from families to football, from animals to ghosts. The books are written by some of the most famous and popular of today's children's authors, and by some of the best new talents, too.

Whether you read one chapter a night, or devour the whole book in one sitting, you'll love Young Corgi books. The more you read, the more you'll want to read!

Other Young Corgi books to get your teeth into:
ZEUS ON THE LOOSE by John Dougherty
BILLY AND THE SEAGULLS by Paul May
TILLY MINT TALES by Berlie Doherty
THE PROMPTER by Chris D'Lacey

ROBOMUM

For Freddie – with love and apologies

ROBOMUM
A YOUNG CORGI BOOK 9780552547369

Published in Great Britain by Corgi Books,
an imprint of Random House Children's Books

This edition published 2003

7 9 10 8 6

The Random House Group Limited makes every effort to ensure
that the papers used in its books are made from trees that have been
legally sourced from well-managed and credibly certified forests.
Our paper procurement policy can be found at:
www.randomhouse.co.uk/paper.htm

Set in 17/21 pt Bembo Schoolbook

Corgi Books are published by Random House Children's Books,
61–63 Uxbridge Road, London W5 5SA,
a division of The Random House Group Ltd

Addresses for Random House Group Ltd companies outside the UK
can be found at: www.randomhouse.co.uk/offices.htm

THE RANDOM HOUSE GROUP Limited Reg. No. 954009
www.**kids**at**randomhouse**.co.uk

A CIP catalogue record for this book is available
from the British Library.

Printed and bound in Great Britain by
Cox & Wyman Ltd, Reading, Berkshire

Mixed Sources
Product group from well-managed
forests and other controlled sources
www.fsc.org Cert no. TT-COC-2139
© 1996 Forest Stewardship Council
FSC

ROBOMUM

Emily Smith

Illustrated by Georgie Birkett

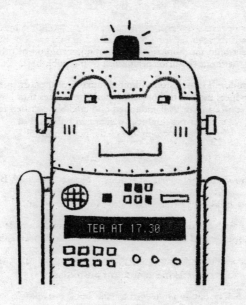

TEA AT 17.30

YOUNG CORGI

My mum is different from other mums. She is sort of brilliant. And she is sort of totally stupid at the same time.

I'll explain.

Mum is fantastic with computers, and works with robots and stuff at this huge company. Half the time she thinks in equations: $x = square$

$root\ of\ z\ plus\ y$, that sort of thing. Did I say she thinks in equations half the time? You'd better make that three-quarters of the time. Four-fifths . . . ?

But . . . Mum is not good at *life*. Ordinary things.

Where shall I start?

Yes. Food. Mum hasn't *quite* worked out that when you run out of food it's a good idea to go and buy some more. I mean, I like boiled eggs and soldiers, I do. But I reckon I've eaten *armies* of the things!

Clothes shopping is not a strong point either. I wear things till the buttons pop. And then I go on wearing them. (The popped-button look is not a good one, believe me.)

And Mum's record on things like clothes-washing or form-filling or fridge-defrosting is — how shall I put it? — a bit hit and miss.

If there was a practical exam for mums, I'm afraid my mum would fail it. I mean, mega fail it. The big "F".

I sometimes wish Mum were more like Mrs Snelling. Mrs Snelling is the super-mum at our school. You know the sort. Slim, neat, well-dressed — and very, very organized. Not a hair out of place, not a minute late at the school gate, not a— Well, you get the picture.

So what do I do when Mum is hopeless?

Sometimes I take no notice. Sometimes I laugh. Sometimes I nag. And sometimes . . . watch out!

One day *everything* went wrong:

First of all Mum lost her wallet so

I couldn't take in a cheque for the school trip (which annoyed Mrs Gibbs).

Halfway through school I realized Mum had forgotten to wash my PE kit and I had to raid Bob Johnson's. (But his shorts fell down – he's bigger than me – and Ianthe Snelling sniggered.)

When I got home, I found my brilliant mother had failed to video the film I wanted. And what had she got instead? Golf.

Golf? *Golf?* GOLF? It was the last straw. I saw *red*. "Mum!" I raged. "You get everything wrong! *Everything!*"

Mum put a hand to her head. "Sorry," she said. "I've been so busy at—"

"You're hopeless!" I yelled.

Mum winced. "Well, maybe I've got one or two things wrong . . ."

"One or two things?" I echoed. "*One or two things?*" And I started listing each and every thing she had got wrong. (OK, I'm not proud of myself, but that's what I did.)

And suddenly Mum got cross. And *she* started shouting. "Just hang on a moment, James!" she yelled. "What do you think I am? A robot? A robot mother? Is that what you want? A *Robomum*?"

And suddenly we looked at each other.

Chapter Two

If anyone else talked about a "Robomum", they'd be making a joke. That's all.

Not my mum. Oh, no. When Mum started talking about a Robomum, that was exactly what she meant. A *Robomum*.

Within seconds of having the idea, she was away. "We'll adapt an M-three!" she said, eyes shining. "We'll need at least twenty gigabytes of memory."

"But, Mum—"

"It'll do all the washing and

cooking and shopping – everything! All the bits I'm no good at! You'll have to recharge it sometimes, that's all!"

"Er, Mum . . ." I said.

Mum beamed. "So, it's all decided then!"

"Well . . ." I thought about it. Perhaps it *would* be nice to have things organized for a change. After all, a robot would be even more efficient than Mrs Snelling! And a real robot around . . . how cool would that be?

"OK," I said.

The Robomum was delivered three weeks later. (When it's anything to do with work, Mum is always dead efficient. She managed to get me a fully working robot – but forgot to buy light bulbs. Again.)

It – she – was amazing.

The way she *looked* was amazing. The way she *moved* was amazing. The way she *spoke* was amazing.

"Greetings, Sentient James!" she pinged.

"Er . . . hello," I said.

"I am your Robomum, Sentient James. My prime directives are fully functional."

I gulped.

14

"That means she's working," said Mum.

"Oh, good," I said weakly. "But why does she call me Sentient James?"

"Oh, that just means she knows you're human. Tell her to stop it if you want."

"How?"

"Speak to her!"

I bit my lip. "Robomum?"

"Yes, Sentient James?"

"You don't have to call me Sentient James. Just James will do."

"Understood. Just James." Lights flashed on the Robomum's front panel. "Data override completed!"

"And now I'll leave you to it!" Mum grabbed her coat. "I've got to get on with my docking system. It has to be accurate to twenty decimal places," she said, doing up her buttons all wrong.

She shut the door.

And there I was. Minus one mother. Plus one Robomum.

The Robomum turned a complete circle, then said in her pingy voice,

"Household chores beginning."
She began.

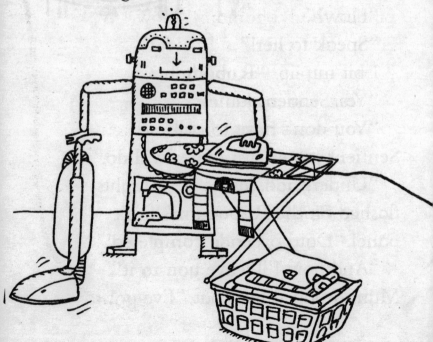

The ironing . . . *pssssss!*

The mending . . . *zzzzzzzt!*

The hoovering . . . *neeyaaaaaah!*

The cleaning-the-kitchen-floor . . . *sloosh!*

The getting-off-bits-of-sandwich-that-were-stuck-on-the-sandwich-toaster . . . *tacka, tacka, tacka, tacka, tacka!*

Soon the house was spotless.

"Household chores completed!" pinged the Robomum. "Now I enter child-play mode." Her lights started flashing. "Choose a game, Just James."

We played noughts and crosses.

The Robomum won.

We played boxes.

The Robomum won.

We played Snap.

The Robomum won.

We played hangman.

The Robomum won. This felt strange as my mum *never* lets me lose at hangman. She gives the little figure buttons or an umbrella if I keep guessing the wrong letters. But the Robomum stuck right to the rules. Oh, yes.

"Would you like to play noughts

and crosses again?" pinged the Robomum. "If you like, Just James, I can program myself to lose."

"Er . . . don't bother," I said.

"What about a game of chess?" she asked.

"No!" I wailed.

Her lights flashed for a bit. "In that case, I shall put myself out of child-play mode – and into shopping mode."

My mouth fell open. "Shopping?" I said.

"Shopping," said the Robomum.

I gulped. This was all going too fast for me. "Shopping for what?"

A quick flash of lights. "Light bulbs, for a start."

And suddenly I realized this was all for real. I was going shopping with the Robomum!

Chapter Three

Three of us went to the shops.

There was me – on feet. There was
our tartan shopper – on little wheels.
And there was the Robomum – on
something else . . .

We got a few funny looks. But most people didn't take much notice.

As we got near the supermarket, the Robomum started on about her "recipe directory".

"What?" I said in rather a tired way.

"I have an in-built directory of five thousand recipes," she said. "Mention a dish that you like, and I will buy the ingredients and prepare it."

Suddenly I stopped feeling so tired. "Apple strudel!" I cried. "I love apple strudel!"

The lights flashed. "Pastry and apple dish originating in Austria. List of ingredients: flour, salt, apples . . ."

The tartan shopper said nothing.

"Greetings, sentient check-out operator!" the Robomum said politely as we got to the check-out.

The man gave us a funny look, but started putting things through.

The Robomum wasn't finished, though. "According to my weighing apparatus, this bag of sugar is under weight by one hundred and eighty-six grams. This, I calculate, is more than the allowed error of plus or minus five per cent."

There was silence.

The man looked at me. His look said, Get it out of here.

I did.

On the way back I was feeling pretty chirpy. After all, it's not everyone who goes shopping with a billion-byte robot. An *apple-strudel-making* billion-byte robot.

I got the Robomum to push the shopper, and ran on ahead. I even started jumping over the chains that marked the parking area. A mistake.

I jumped over the first chain. *Wheesh!*

I jumped over the second chain. *Wheesh!*

I jumped over the third chain. *Wheesh!*

I jumped over the fourth chain, caught my foot, and – arms waving – fell onto the concrete. *Whump!*

Ooof, it was painful! Blood sprang from my knee.

As I lay on the ground, shocked and groaning, I saw the Robomum standing close by. Her beady eyes were on me. "What did you do that for?" she said.

I didn't answer.

"You misjudged the height of the chain by four point five centimetres, which—"

"Shut up," I groaned. "I'm in pain! I've hurt my knee!"

"Well, the pain should decrease slowly over the next ten minutes."

"Great!" I muttered.

I sat there miserably. A Robomum wasn't much good for this sort of thing. This was the sort of thing you wanted a proper mum for. But right then Mum had her head stuck in a program for a space-shuttle docking system . . .

Somehow I staggered back. The Robomum washed my knee and put a plaster on it. I still felt very sorry for myself. "I can't do much with this knee," I said, dropping onto the sofa. "I think I'd better just sit here and watch telly."

The Robomum's lights flashed for a few seconds. Then she said, "This will make you pleased, Just James. I have found something it is possible for you to do with a sore leg."

"What?" I said grumpily.

"Your recorder practice."

"*My recorder practice?* But I haven't done any for weeks!"

"Exactly," said the Robomum. "And I have perfect pitch."

Chapter Four

It was the end of school. We were in
the corridor outside our classroom,
getting ready to go. My friend Eddie
was complaining about the amount
of Maths homework. My friend
Eddie is always complaining about
the amount of Maths homework.

Suddenly Mrs Gibbs came charging through the swing doors. "No one leave the premises!" she shouted. "Mrs McPhipps's orders!"

There were mutters of excitement. Ianthe Snelling burst into tears about being late for extra French.

"Why?" asked someone. "What's up?"

Mrs Gibbs frowned. "Well, there's something strange . . . in the playground."

"Must be Mrs McPhipps!" joked Eddie

"No . . . it's some sort of machine!" said Mrs Gibbs.

Eddie grabbed me by the arm. "Hey, James! Maybe it's something to do with that new robot of yours!"

I yelped. "Mrs Gibbs?"

"Yes, James?"

"Is it . . . a sort of robot? With flashing lights and a funny voice?"

"Yes, James. Why?"

"Er . . . I think it may be something to do with me."

She flung an arm towards the exit. "Well, get out there!"

I started for the swing doors.

"James?"

I stopped. "Yes? "

Mrs Gibbs gave me the eye. "Stay in school unless you're sure it's safe. OK?"

"OK, Mrs Gibbs!" And I was off again.

I ran to the main entrance, and peered through the glass doors. Sure enough, there was the Robomum.

I slipped out onto the steps. She was standing on one side of the playground – and the mums and dads and little kids were standing on the other.

Suddenly I saw that if you didn't know the Robomum was safe, she might look quite frightening.

The mums and dads certainly looked worried, but some of the kids were enjoying themselves no end.

"It's an alien!" cried one.

"It's a dustbin!" said another.

"It's a combine harvester!" said another.

"I reckon it's a terminator," said a red-haired girl grimly.

There was silence. And then someone said, "What do you mean, *terminator*?"

"Something what *terminates* people," said the red-haired girl. "I reckon it's got a laser what'll slice us like butter!"

"I don't want to be terminated!" howled a little boy.

"I don't want to be sliced like butter!" howled another little boy.

The Robomum seemed to have heard this. She flashed her lights and turned her speakers up. "I am not a terminator, except in the case of certain household pests!" she boomed. "I am programmed to recognize the young male human known as Just James Sullivan, and escort him back to number thirty-three, Plaistow Avenue, stopping at roads where . . ."

As the Robomum pinged on,

Mrs McPhipps came up to me. She looked harassed. Even more harassed than usual. "Is this machine really something to do with you, James?"

"Yes," I said, and I tried to explain. It wasn't very easy somehow.

"But really, James!" Mrs McPhipps interrupted in horror. "A robot is no substitute for a *mother*!"

"No, no, no!" I said. "She just does the bits my mum is useless at!"

"Like what?"

"Er . . . most things, really."

Mrs McPhipps frowned. "Well, it's most irregular!" she said. "I wish your mother had said something."

Mrs Snelling, who was standing near by, shook her head. "Really!" she said. "Leaving a child in the care of a walking hoover!"

"Oh, she's more than a hoover!" I said eagerly. "She can do everything. She shops and cooks and irons everything – even my pants! And she cleans the whole house in seconds! She listens to my reading book and she never gets bored, even if it's a really boring one!"

"Hmmm!" said Mrs McPhipps, suddenly thoughtful. I thought she was impressed about the boring

reading books, but it wasn't that.
"Cleans the whole house in seconds, you say?"

"Yes."

"Well, James, I've had an idea."

"Oh?"

"I've got two cleaners off sick. And it's Open Evening soon. And the school needs a really good clean . . ."

I had to agree. It was the least we could do after all the bother we had caused.

Mrs McPhipps started leading the Robomum into school to show her where to start.

One of the little kids pointed excitedly. "Look, the terminator is taking Mrs McPhipps off!"

"It's going to slice her like butter!"

"Or take her hostage!"

"Or both!"

"Save Mrs McPhipps!"

"All rush at the same time!"

No one rushed.

As they got to the main door, the Robomum turned and faced the crowd. Everyone fell silent. "Greetings, sentient mothers and fathers!" she pinged. "Greetings, sentient children." There was a flourish of lights on her front. "I am about to clean your

school. I shall do my best to empty
your litter bins, wash all surfaces and
remove any unwanted matter from
your lavatories." She turned and went
through the doors.

"I told you it wasn't a combine
harvester," said the red-haired girl.

Three hours later the school was
spotless. The kitchen shone like the
inside of a spaceship. Every single
book in every single classroom was in
alphabetical order. And even the loos
looked quite respectable.

The Robomum had even gone to work on Mrs McPhipps. She gave her "the best back-rub of a lifetime".

Mrs McPhipps waved us off in a happy daze.

Chapter Five

"So how's it going with your robot?" said Mum. The Robomum was on charge, and we were clearing away supper.

"Not bad!" I said cheerfully. I had just had three helpings of the Robomum's chocolate mousse.

"How do you find her as company?" said Mum, putting the butter in the oven. I took the butter out of the oven and put it in the fridge. "Well, she never gets tired or cross, which is good . . ."

"Yes."

"And she never shouts at me, which is good . . ."

"Yes."

"But . . ."

"But what?"

I tried to think. "Well, she's not like a person."

"No," said Mum. "She wouldn't be."

"And when she makes me do recorder practice, she's accurate . . . but no fun."

"Hmm." Mum frowned. "Yes, I do see. How could we make her more fun?"

I thought. "Well... I suppose she

could sort of make
jokes and things."

Mum nodded.
"Right. Jokes it is!
I'll scan some
into her database
at once."

So the
Robomum
started making jokes.
Non-stop in her pingy drone. She
started before breakfast, and went on
and on and on until bedtime. The
jokes were about everything from
aardvarks to zebras, but they had one
thing in common. They were terrible!

"*How do you service a pogo stick?
Give it a spring clean.*

"*What is yellow and flickers? A lemon
with a loose connection.*

"*What word is always pronounced
wrong? Wrong.*

"What time is it when an elephant . . .?

"What did the bishop . . .?

"Knock, knock . . ."

It was dire.

I had to hide in my room.

Once I had to go to the bathroom in the middle of the night. Just as I groped my way to the loo, the Robomum burst in!

"What's grey with a big trunk? A mouse going on holiday.

"Why do the French eat snails? Because they don't like fast food.

"Two fat men ran a race. One ran in short bursts, the other in burst shorts."

Believe me, this is not what I needed just then.

I woke Mum early next morning. "I've changed my mind about the jokes."

She blinked sleepily at me. "No jokes?"

I shook my head. "No jokes."

"OK," said Mum.

When I got to school, Eddie said, "Hey, James, heard this one? I read it on my cereal packet. *Why did the skeleton go to the—?*"

"No!" I cried.

"All right," said Eddie. "How about this one, then? *What do you call a man—?*"

"*No!*" I screamed.

Eddie looked at me oddly. "I thought you had a sense of humour."

"I have," I said. "But not for jokes."

He frowned. "So what else is there?"

I thought. "Well, Eddie, your Albert Einstein impression always makes me laugh."

So Eddie did his Albert Einstein impression all the way through geography, and got a detention.

Chapter Six

Eddie and I raced down the road.
School was over for the day, and
Eddie was coming to tea. We had just
been looking in a video shop window
and the Robomum was waiting for
us by a lamppost (the Robomum
never ever minded waiting).

45

When we reached her, there was a strange blue light flashing.

"Are you all right, Robomum?" I asked.

"I don't know, Just James," said the Robomum. "I hope the urine won't corrode my metal."

What? Eddie and I stared at each other. Had the Robomum blown a fuse? "What are you talking about, Robomum?"

The lights flashed again. "Someone just came up and urinated on me," she said.

"Urinated? What – you mean, *weed* on you?"

A flash of lights. "That's another expression, yes."

We stared down. Sure enough, there was something dribbling down her metal skirt.

Eddie shook his head. "What a

world, when someone does that to a strange robot."

"But who was it?" I said. "What did he look like?"

"He was short," said the Robomum. "With dark curly hair."

"What was he wearing?"

"A collar," said the Robomum.

"What else?"

"Nothing else," said the Robomum. "Just a collar."

Eddie and I looked around nervously. Where was this person wearing nothing but a collar?

Suddenly Eddie started laughing. "How . . . how many legs did he have, Robomum?"

I stared at him. Now I thought *Eddie* had blown a fuse!

"Four," said the Robomum.

"Four?" I cried. My mind wasn't working very fast.

"Don't you see, thicko?" Eddie was laughing even harder now. "It was a dog!"

"Oh." I turned on the Robomum indignantly. "Why didn't you say it was a dog?"

"You never asked, Just James!" said the Robomum.

"Come on," said Eddie. "Let's take the Robomum back and wipe her down."

"That is a most intelligent suggestion, Sentient Eddie," said the Robomum.

"Thank you, Robomum!" Eddie grinned at her. "And you needn't say Sentient Eddie any more. Just call me – Wonderful Eddie!"

And the Robomum did. All the way home. Eddie kept asking her stupid questions (and he can ask very stupid questions), just to hear her call him Wonderful Eddie. I began to feel tired . . .

When we got back I didn't feel like kicking a football around. Nor, when tea came, did I feel like the Robomum's veggieburgers.

"Eat up, James, these burgers are fantastic!" Eddie munched away in a most annoying way.

"They're not as good as usual," I said crossly.

The Robomum trundled over — then suddenly shot out an arm.

"Oi!" I said. "Stop it!"

 But the Robomum had something pressed to my forehead. Some lights flashed, and then she spoke. "I believe Just James is malfunctioning," she said.

Wonderful Eddie laughed. I was so furious, I kicked her. *Clang!* But of course the Robomum was right. In her terms I *was* malfunctioning. I was ill.

I was really quite ill. I felt wobbly (legs), sore (throat) and hot (everywhere). Eddie disappeared (though not before finishing off a second veggieburger), and I climbed, groaning, into bed.

"Liquids!" pinged the Robomum, looking down at me.

"What?" I said crossly.

"You need to drink a lot of liquids." And she swept off and came back a few seconds later with a glass of orange juice.

I lay there, sipping my orange juice and feeling sorry for myself. I lay there for what seemed a long time . . .

Then the door opened. I thought it was the Robomum again.

"James?" said a voice.

I looked up. It was my mum.

Mum took two days off work. OK, a lot of the time she was tapping on her laptop and stuff, but she was at home. That was cool. A robot's temperature-gauge may be more accurate than a mum's hand on the forehead, but it certainly doesn't feel as good.

The day after Mum went back to work, there was a ring at the door – followed quickly by a loud knock, then another ring. A few seconds later I heard the Robomum trill, "Greetings, Wonderful Eddie!"

"Way to go, Robomum!" cried Eddie, and I heard the sound of a hand smacking on metal. Soon the Robomum's voice pinged up the stairs, "Wonderful Eddie is coming up to visit Just James. He brings half a kilogram of grapes." There was a pause. "Wonderful Eddie has picked two of the grapes and is eating them."

I heard steps on the stairs, and then Eddie bounded in. "Hi, James!" he said. "You don't look very ill."

"No," I said. "I'm nearly better."

Eddie dropped the grapes on the bed. "Mum sent these. They're supposed to be seedless, but look!" And he spat a pip at me.

OK, Eddie may not know much about visiting the sick, but he is my friend and I was pleased to see him. "So what's up?" I said. "What's happened at school?"

Eddie munched some more grapes. "Not a lot."

"Something *must* have happened."

Eddie thought. "Erm . . . Ianthe Snelling jumped on the desks and got a detention."

I gaped at him. "*No!*"

Eddie frowned. "Come to think of it, that wasn't her, that was me."

"Oh."

We played a fantasy card game, but Eddie started arguing about the rules, and we stopped. Then Eddie glanced at his watch, and said he had to go. "Well, make sure you're back at school next week!" he said, getting up.

"Why next week?" I said.

"It's the swimming gala, of course!"

"Oh. Yes."

Eddie whirled his arms and grinned. "And you wouldn't want to miss Wonderful Eddie doing his wonderful butterfly, would you?"

A few seconds later I heard the door slam.

"Wonderful Eddie has left the building!" announced the Robomum.

Chapter Seven

On Sunday morning I really did feel
better. So the Robomum and I went
along to the shops for the papers and
some chocolate milk.

On the way back the Robomum
suddenly said, "There is a smell!"

She was right. There *was* a smell.
A nasty burning smell. A few steps
later I saw why.

Just ahead of us was a block of
flats. Black smoke was billowing from
a top-floor window. Some people
were gathered round the main
entrance. There was a boy a bit
younger than me, wearing pyjamas
and trainers. Beside him a little girl
was huddled in a duvet. And there

were quite a few adults as well.

"A fire!" I said. "Looks as if those people have escaped!"

We came up alongside. A woman in an anorak was coughing.

"It's that smoke that does it!" a man in a tracksuit was saying. "Gets to your lungs."

"Lucky you got out so quick!" said someone.

The woman in the anorak nodded. I noticed she was shivering – even though it was quite a warm day.

"Fire service should be here any minute," said someone else.

Suddenly the boy in pyjamas gave a loud gasp. "Ernest and Ethel!" he cried. "We've left Ernest and Ethel!"

Everyone froze.

The boy started running back towards the flat, but the man in the tracksuit grabbed him. "You can't do it, son!" he said. "No one can. The smoke would kill you."

And then the boy started crying. "Ethel and Ernest!" he sobbed. "They'll die!"

The woman in the anorak put an arm round him. "There, there," she said. "We'll get you some more."

"They won't be the same!" cried
the boy. "I want Ethel and Ernest."

He was howling now. "They're
mine and . . . and they trusted me!"

We walked on by. I couldn't bear
to stand and stare (as some people
were starting to do). I felt so sorry
for the boy. If only I could do
something . . .

A few metres further on I stopped –
stock still – and yelled two words.

"The Robomum!"

Everyone stopped talking and looked at me.

And then their eyes fell on the Robomum.

And I could see the hope leap in the boy's eyes.

The Robomum took it as calmly as if I had asked her to fetch something from the dry cleaner's. With a brief flurry of lights, she sped into the main entrance, leaving the doors swinging. As soon as I lost sight of her, I began to worry. Could she be damaged by fire? After all, metal will melt at a great heat, won't it? What was I going to tell Mum if her precious robot was destroyed?

The seconds passed, and she didn't reappear. I was getting more and more worried. Surely it was quite a

small flat. The Robomum should
have been out by now! And the black
smoke seemed to be getting worse . . .
Suddenly, the swing doors burst open.
I caught my breath – and the
Robomum trundled through. She
looked a bit blackened, but otherwise
just the same. And in her metal arms
she carried a see-through canister.

I heard the boy gasp, and as she came forward, he ran up to her. We followed and gathered round. Everyone stared down.

Inside the canister, sitting on a small branch, were two green . . . stick insects. They were totally and absolutely still.

No one said anything, but everyone was wondering the same thing. Had the smoke got to them? Were they dead after all? How could you *tell*?

Then suddenly it happened. One of them *waved a front leg*.

The boy started crying and laughing at the same time. And everyone else went mad, and started cheering! And at that moment we heard the fire engine . . .

"That was fantastic, Robomum," I said, as we made for home.

"Yes," said the Robomum. "I know you like chocolate milk."

Chapter Eight

I wasn't allowed to swim in the
end-of-term gala. Mum said it was
too soon after my illness.

In the end I was quite grateful –
for two reasons. The first was that
actually I *did* still feel a bit wobbly.
The second was that I got a good
view of the whole thing.

I saw Eddie come third in his
butterfly (not quite as wonderful as
he hoped). But – more importantly –
I got a good look at Mrs Snelling.
Busy, efficient, organized
Mrs Snelling. The Mrs Snelling I
had always thought was so
marvellous. And the scales fell
from my eyes.

There she was, chatting up Mr Greig the PE teacher.

There she was, hissing last-minute instructions to her children.

There she was, bossing other mums around the tea.

And when Paul Snelling didn't win the back crawl, she complained about *the lane bobbles*!

I sat there on my orange plastic seat, and – *ta-ra!* – I saw the light. Mrs Snelling might be busy and efficient and organized, but she was a pushy mother to end all pushy mothers – and a pain in the neck. And being organized isn't everything, anyway. Now I saw why Ianthe was such a drip.

And no sooner had I seen the light,
than an amazing thing happened.
It was Mr Greig's fault, really.

It was nearly time for tea, and he
needed to tell her. But he should
never have called out, "Someone
grab Mrs Snelling!" Not in the
Robomum's hearing anyway.

Someone did grab Mrs Snelling.

It was the Robomum.

She thought "grab" meant "grab"
– and she "grabbed". "Greetings,
Sentient Mrs Snelling!" she pinged,
as she picked her up in her
metal arms.

It was a wonderful sight. You can
say this for Mum's company – they
certainly make a good strong robot.
Some of the kids started laughing –
and I saw one or two parents
trying to hide smiles. "Let me go!"
shouted Mrs Snelling, struggling.

And that was a mistake. A big
mistake.

The Robomum did let her go –
right over the side of the pool.

Splash!

I looked at Ianthe Snelling. And do you know? She didn't burst into tears. She went and helped her mum out of the pool. There may be some hope for the girl yet . . .

Chapter Nine

The Robomum and I made our way
happily home. But as soon as we let
ourselves in, I saw something strange.
Mum's laptop was sitting on the table
in the hall. She must be back already.
But why? My heart missed a beat.
Was she ill? Had something happened
at work?

But then she called out from the front room, "James? I'm in here!"

I ran in to find her sprawled on the sofa. In the window was a massive bunch of flowers. And on the coffee table in front of Mum was a tray of champagne and other goodies.

"Hey, Mum!" I said. "What's all this?"

She looked at me and smiled. "I've done it."

I looked at her. "You mean . . . ?"

She nodded. "The docking system."

"It docks?"

"It docks."

I smiled. "You rock!"

Mum laughed. "I rock!" She waved a hand round the room. "My bosses sent me all this. That sparkling apple juice was for you, but I've started it." She picked up a glass, and sipped. "Delicious!"

I poured myself some apple juice, and raised my glass to her. "To a brilliant mum!" I said. "I'm proud of you!" And I *was* proud of her. She might not be good at ordinary things, but she is very good at extraordinary things – like robots.

She laughed again. "Well, thanks for being so understanding these last few weeks."

"Mmm." I felt a bit embarrassed – sometimes I hadn't been *so* understanding. "The Robomum helped a lot."

Mum nodded. "She'd better go back now."

"Really?"

"Yup." Mum sipped her apple juice. "She was only on loan while I finished the docking project. And I'm going to be at home a lot more now."

My heart leapt. "Great!"

I thought about it. Yes, I would miss the Robomum's cooking. And the clean house, and everything. But she didn't compare with my mum. Even when my mum was only half with-it …

★

"Goodbye, then!" I said to the Robomum three days later, patting her metal arm.

"Goodbye, Just James!" she pinged.

"Your chocolate cake was the greatest!" I said.

"Remark filed in Compliments/ Catering Section!" Her lights flashed. "I've added a lot to my database, working with you and Wonderful Eddie!" she said.

Then off she went in a van. I watched it drive away, feeling sad. Surprisingly sad. After all, she was only a machine – less alive than Ernest and Ethel. She wasn't even a "she" either. She was an "it".

Just as the van turned the corner, the phone went. Mum went into the front room to answer it. I heard her gasp, "But that's a huge project! Anyway, I've just promised . . ."

I wasn't really listening. I was more interested in going to the kitchen to see if the Robomum had left us anything for supper. I opened the fridge. It was empty.
Very clean – but empty.

A few minutes later I heard Mum's voice. "James?" she called.

I walked into the front room to find her standing there with a strange expression on her face.

I stared at her. "What is it, Mum? What's wrong?"

"Nothing's wrong." Mum looked slightly dazed. "But I've just been offered this amazing project. With a completely new type of robot."

"Oh." I looked down at the bottle of champagne she had been given for the last project. It hadn't even been opened yet.

Mum took my hand, and drew me to the sofa. For a few seconds she was silent. Then she looked at me. "It's your choice, James. I really mean it."

"My choice? What do you mean, my choice?"

She put a hand to my face. "Well, it's like this. The people who want me to do this new thing *really* want me to do it. I said at first that I couldn't, but they've said they'll wait. Four weeks."

I met her eyes. "Four weeks?"

"Yup. And in that time we can do some great stuff together, you and me. You break up soon, remember. We'll have great fun." She squeezed my knee. "But then it would be me back to work."

I nodded.

She drew a breath. "And if you really don't want me to do this project I won't. I promised, and I don't break my promises."

I looked at her. It was *so* difficult. I wanted my mum to myself for a good long time. Chaotic though she was, in the really really important things, she was a good mother. I knew that now.

But I also knew how much she loved her work . . .

Suddenly I made my decision. "You do it, Mum!"

"Oh, James!" She put her arms round me and hugged me tight.

Then I had a thought. "But can I have the Robomum back?"

Mum laughed in my ear. "Of course you can – Wonderful James!"

THE END

ANNIE AND THE ALIENS
Emily Smith

Watch out!
There's an alien in the garden!

Annie is furious. Her brothers have
banned her from their room and insist
on keeping secrets from her. But
Annie won't be left out. When she
finds out what the boys are
whispering about, they'll get an
astronomical surprise!

An entertaining story from the
author of *The Shrimp* (Smarties
Gold Medal-winner) and *Astrid,
the Au Pair from Outer Space*
(Smarties Silver Medal-winner)

ISBN 0 552 54829 4

YOUNG CORGI